DAVID BEDFORD

Illustrated by Keith Brumpton

LITTLE HARE

Chapter 1

"It's on!" whispered Harvey as Darren, who had just arrived at school, sat down next to him.

Darren ducked behind a large book with a picture of a rocket on the front, and said, "What is?"

Harvey glanced towards the front of the classroom, where Mr Spottiwoode, their teacher, was standing, his mouth moving lazily under his moustache as he began writing Tuesday's work on the board.

Harvey said excitedly in Darren's ear, "The Floodlights Cup!"

"The *what*?!" Darren said loudly, sitting straight up.

"Sshhh!" hissed Harvey, dragging him down again and looking anxiously towards Mr Spottiwoode, who was now blowing his nose noisily. Harvey watched him tuck his hanky back inside his pocket, then begin talking. It sounded like his usual speech — something about trying harder and doing better. Harvey turned back to Darren and said, "You know how they're putting floodlights on our pitch this week?"

"Yeah," said Darren eagerly, nodding for Harvey to go on.

"Well," said Harvey, "to celebrate, there's going to be an evening match."

Darren's eyes widened.

"And," Harvey continued, "the winners get a silver Floodlights Cup!"

Darren's eyes nearly popped out of his skull. "A silver cup!"

Harvey knew exactly how Darren was feeling. The Team had never won a cup before. They had only received a certificate for coming top of the league last season.

"Rita told me about it last night," Harvey explained. "Her dad is helping to organise it. There's a big cup that The Team holds for a year, with our name engraved on it, and medals for each of us to keep. If we win, that is."

"We will," said Darren determinedly. "Who are we playing?"

Harvey smoothed out a piece of paper. "I wrote it down," he said, showing it to Darren.

"Finbar Fly's All Stars," read Darren in a puzzled voice. "Who are they?"

"Never heard of them," said Harvey, grinning.

"Finbar Fly!" snorted Darren. "They sound second rate. No, *third* rate." He turned to face Harvey. "Looks like The Team are finally going to win a cup!"

Harvey nodded happily. A team they'd never even heard of wasn't likely to be a problem.

"When do we get our silverware?" said Darren.

"Saturday night," said Harvey. "After the game."

Darren spent the rest of Tuesday asking Harvey questions. How big were the medals? Was the cup completely silver, or was there some gold in it, too? And would all their names be engraved on it, or just "The Team"?

Harvey did his best to answer. They could talk easily that afternoon because their teacher had taken them into the playground to pull on a giant elastic band. Mr Spottiwoode held on to one end, and one by one the class pulled on the other end.

"Why are we doing this?" asked Darren, straining, when it was his turn.

"Dunno," said Harvey.

Back in the classroom, Harvey hurriedly packed up, and as soon as the bell went he pushed towards the door.

"Mr Boots!"

Harvey swivelled around. His teacher was beckoning him over.

As Harvey made his way to Mr Spottiwoode's desk, he noticed that everyone else was clutching a white envelope. Darren was eyeing his worriedly.

"Do you even know what these are about?" Mr Spottiwoode asked him sternly.

"Er, of course," said Harvey. "I mean, no. Sorry."

"I've told the class about a dozen times!" Mr Spottiwoode pursed his lips and his moustache stood out like a tiny umbrella.

"Oh, yeah. That. Now I remember," said Harvey, trying to sound convincing.

Mr Spottiwoode sighed as he handed Harvey an envelope. *For the Attention of Mr and Mrs Boots*, read Harvey.

"Uh, thanks," he said.

Together, he and Darren headed for the school gate. Darren was already tearing paper.

"Is that for you?" said Harvey, surprised.

"It's for my folks," admitted Darren. "But I always read my reports first, so I can warn them."

"Reports?" said Harvey. He read over Darren's shoulder, "Mid-term Report".

Underneath there was a list of the topics they'd been studying in class, followed by comments from Mr Spottiwoode. Every one of the comments was, "Satisfactory".

"Phew!" said Darren with relief. "That *is* satisfying! Go on, Harvey, open yours. *You* haven't got anything to worry about — your report is always better than mine."

Harvey opened his envelope carefully so that he could seal it again. Then he gasped.

Next to every topic, Mr Spottiwoode had scrawled the same word in thick black ink. *"Failing."* But it was what his teacher had written at the bottom of the page that really set Harvey's heart pounding.

"Harvey's normally high standards have taken a dive. He **must** concentrate in lessons! I recommend that he be banned from playing soccer until his school work improves.

Yours sincerely,

F. Spottiwoode."

Harvey could hardly breathe. He felt as if he'd just been winded by a crunching tackle. Silently, he handed his report to Darren.

Darren's mouth dropped open. "What about the Floodlights Cup?"

Harvey felt a lump rising in his throat.

"Harvey," cried Darren, "you can't play. You're *banned*!"

Chapter 2

Harvey walked up Baker Street in a daze, hardly aware that Darren was following him. He wished he didn't have to go home. He knew that as soon as his mum and dad read his report they'd do exactly what Mr Spottiwoode had recommended. He'd be banned from playing for The Team.

"I know that I talk a lot," said Darren apologetically. "I can't help it. But we do still listen sometimes, don't we?"

"You do," said Harvey, morosely. The truth was, he'd been dreaming up some new moves for The Team, and when he wasn't listening to Darren, he liked to run through the moves in his head and imagine how they'd turn out. "I've been daydreaming," he admitted. "It's my own fault."

Harvey ground to a halt beside the gate to Professor Gertie's inventing tower. He heard a whirring noise, and looked up.

Professor Gertie, who was Harvey's next-door neighbour, was dangling from a rope halfway up the tower. She seemed to be riding

a bike, knitting, *and* trying to clean a window with a sponge the size of a dinner table.

"Yoo-hoo!" she called, pedalling madly as she coasted to the ground. The wheels skidded on the grass and Professor Gertie slipped off the bike, landing with a *sploosh*! on the soapy sponge.

When she stood up, she was soaked from head to foot with dirty water.

"Nice, er, whatever it is!" Harvey heard Rita call from behind him and Darren. She was panting, and Harvey guessed she'd run all the way from her school.

"For your information," Professor Gertie told Rita, "that's my latest invention: a Chore All. I can use it to do my two least favourite jobs at once — cleaning dirty windows and de-holing socks."

"What's the bicycle for?" asked Darren curiously.

"Pedalling provides the lifting force, of course!" Professor Gertie said briskly, as if that part was obvious. Harvey had no idea what she was talking about.

"Now then," Professor Gertie said, noticing Harvey's glum expression. "What's up with you?"

Without a word, Harvey handed her his report, and she and Rita read it together.

Professor Gertie's face turned the colour of beetroot. "Rats on fire!" she fumed. "Can teachers really do that?"

"Not at my school," said Rita. "The worst grade they give is a W."

"A what?" said Darren.

"It stands for 'Worrying'. They don't say 'Failing' because it might make a person feel useless."

Harvey shrugged. "I don't care what word they use," he said. "If I'm rubbish, I'd rather be told about it."

"We'll have to pull out of the Finbar game," said Darren. Harvey could tell he was trying to hide his disappointment.

"What's a Finbar game?" asked Professor Gertie.

Harvey and Rita quickly explained about the Floodlights Cup.

"It's only a silver cup anyway," Darren said. "There's probably no gold in it."

"The Team can still play," Harvey insisted. "I'm the only one who's banned — no one else should have to miss out."

"But you're our captain!" said Rita, shocked. "The Team needs you!"

"Of course Harvey will play!" snapped Professor Gertie. "I'll find a way, have no fear about that!" Holding Harvey's report in the air, she declared firmly, "Harvey — you're playing!"

Harvey waited hopefully for something to happen, but nothing did.

"How can I?" he said at last.

Suddenly Mark 1, the Football Machine, jumped out of the window of the inventing tower, and landed lightly behind Professor Gertie on his Bouncing Boots. He was her greatest invention, a robot designed purely for football.

"Playyy?" the robot said eagerly in his strange, mechanical voice.

"Not now," Professor Gertie told him impatiently. "I'm trying to think. Anyway," she said, as the smell of pizza filled the air, "it's time for your dinner."

Mark 1's laser eyes flashed red. The robot's head swivelled, his neck stretched, and he opened his mouth.

"Hey!" said Harvey. "Hang on — she didn't mean—"

The metal jaws closed on Harvey's report and tugged it from Professor Gertie's hand.

"Stop!" cried Harvey.

Mark 1 began to chew.

"Spit it out!" said Professor Gertie crossly, taking hold of Mark 1's head and feeling around inside his mouth. "Ouch!" she yelped. "He bit me!"

Mark 1 beeped, and began to swallow. Harvey watched a shape like a ping-pong ball moving down his throat.

Mark 1 burped.

"Where's my report?" said Harvey weakly.

No one answered.

"Oh no!" Professor Gertie suddenly dashed towards the tower door as black smoke began to billow from her kitchen window. "My pepperoni!"

Mark 1 bounced along behind her, beeping like a fire alarm.

Harvey, Rita and Darren followed the robot into Professor Gertie's tower. At the top of the twisting stairway, Harvey noticed that Darren was bent over, holding his stomach. At first Harvey thought he was being sick, but then he realised that Darren was laughing as if he'd just seen the funniest thing in the world.

"That robot!" Darren spluttered. "He's a genius! Now you *can't* show your report to your parents!"

"I know that!" said Harvey angrily. He was beginning to panic. "I'm going to be in even more trouble!"

"No you're not," said Darren. "Think about it, Harvey. This means you're only banned from playing soccer at school, where Mr Spottiwoode can check on you. But there's nothing to stop you playing after school!"

Harvey paused, thinking. He couldn't exactly show the report to his mum and dad now, could he? So he wouldn't be doing anything wrong. Not really.

Harvey felt excitement surge inside him. "Call an extra training session," he told Darren. "The Team are going to be well prepared for the Floodlights Cup."

"We'll have to be," said Rita quietly.

"Why?" said Darren.

"I've found out who Finbar Fly is — that's what I came to tell you." Harvey saw an agonised look pass over Rita's face. "Harvey, Darren — he's your *teacher*."

Chapter 3

"Mr Spottiwoode?" Darren began to cackle. "He's got hands like shovels and feet like a duck! And he's *old* — he must be thirty at least! Spot's All Stars — we'll slaughter them!"

Harvey wasn't smiling, though. He was still watching Rita, who looked deadly serious.

"He's the goalie," Rita said.

Darren looked at her.

"I guess his big hands and feet help him stop the ball," Rita mused. "My dad said he was a legend. The first professional player to come from our town. *And* he's the only goalie ever to have a one hundred percent clean sheet."

"He never let in a single goal?" said Harvey, awestruck.

"That's impossible," Darren said.

"He only played for one season," Rita explained. "Then he quit to become a teacher."

"He gave up being the best goalie ever for that?" said Darren in disbelief. "That can't be right."

"Maybe he was permanently injured," suggested Harvey.

"My dad said he just wanted to be a teacher more than anything else," said Rita. Then her eyes widened. "Hang on!" she said. "Harvey can't play in the Floodlights after all. Mr Spot is the one who banned him!"

"Oh no!" said Darren, putting his hands to his head.

Harvey was stunned.

"He must have been watching you score goals in the playground," said Darren hotly. "He realised you were going to ruin his precious goalkeeping record. That's why he wants you out of the game."

Harvey shook his head doubtfully. "I'm not that good," he said.

"And I don't think a teacher would do that," said Rita reasonably.

"Well this one would," Darren said grimly. "The test proves everything."

"Test?" said Harvey. "What test?"

Darren was amazed. "Don't you listen to *anything* Mr Spot says? On Friday morning we're being tested on every topic we've done this term."

"A test on everything!" said Rita in wonder. "That *is* mean."

Harvey felt his shoulders drooping. First he was banned from playing soccer, and now he had to do a test he could never pass.

Rita looked upset. "What if you study really hard?" she suggested. "Maybe you can do well enough in the test to make your teacher lift the ban."

"Yeah, maybe," said Harvey, trying to sound encouraging.

Darren shook his head gloomily. "Harvey will need to get top marks for Mr Spot to lift the ban," he said. "Let's face it — Finbar Fly's stolen our cup. It's over."

When Harvey left for school on Wednesday morning, there were bags under his eyes and he was yawning. He'd found a geography book beneath his bed, and stayed up late reading. But now, he couldn't remember a single thing about it.

As he walked past Professor Gertie's tower, he spotted a work table at the far end of the garden … With a cry of alarm, he sprinted over.

"What's wrong?" he shouted. "Has there been an accident?"

Mark 1 was lying on the table. Wires were spilling from his shirt like spaghetti, and his head looked like it had been cut off at the mouth.

"Don't worry," said Professor Gertie soothingly. "He's okay." She pressed the button on the robot's chest and he sat up.

Harvey flinched. The top part of Mark 1's head, which had been made from an old flip-top rubbish bin, was dangling down his back, connected by a hinge.

"I'm just doing some much-needed spring cleaning," said Professor Gertie brightly, swinging Mark 1's head back into place with a *click!*

"Hell-lo Harvvv," said the robot, rubbing his chin. Harvey winced as Professor Gertie lifted the lever above Mark 1's eyes and let his head fall back again. *Bonk!*

"Doesn't that hurt?" he said to the upside-down face. Talking to the headless robot made Harvey feel dizzy.

"Itt ticklezz!" said Mark 1 before Professor Gertie detached his head and carried it away.

"How are you, Harvey?" said Professor Gertie, concerned. "Did you sort out your problems with Mr Spotty?"

"I've got to pass a test," said Harvey.

"That won't be a problem for you!" said Professor Gertie confidently.

"There's a lot to learn, though," said Harvey. "And I've only got two days."

Professor Gertie just winked at him. "Forty-eight hours is plenty of time. Believe me, Harvey, you'll be fine. Between you and me," she said, lowering her voice and walking Harvey a few paces from the robot, "you're even a match for Mark 1, you know. Your passing is almost perfect, your goal-scoring is excellent, and your tactics are more clever than you realise. Harvey, you're a *leader*."

"But that's *soccer*," said Harvey. "Our test is on everything we do at *school*."

"I have complete faith in you, Harvey," said the professor absently. She bent over and began to poke inside Mark 1's rubbish-bin skull. She picked out an old bird's nest. "No wonder he's getting woolly-headed! Honestly, Harvey — Mark 1 may be the most brilliant robot ever invented, but he can't even remember to tie his bootlaces. Apart from coaching The Team, he doesn't do a single useful thing. And he eats *anything*!"

She pulled out a tangle of fishing line, a handful of sparkly sweet wrappers, and four marbles.

Harvey saw something else. Reaching in carefully, he squeezed it between his finger and thumb and tugged it free. It was covered with fluff.

"You missed this," he said. "I think it's a dried pea."

"Not quite," said the professor. "That's a Pea *Brain!*"

Harvey nearly dropped it. "It's a *what?*"

"It's Mark 1's control centre." Professor Gertie took the Pea Brain from Harvey, blew it clean, and put it back into Harvey's hand.

Harvey held it up to his eyes and saw tiny wires, as fine as hairs, sticking out of it.

"Is this all Mark 1 needs?" said Harvey. "To play soccer and everything?"

Professor Gertie nodded proudly.

But Harvey was not impressed. If it only took a brain the size of a pea to be a soccer genius, what did Harvey have inside his own head?

I bet I've got a Pea Brain too, he told himself miserably. And it won't be much use for a test on every topic in two days' time.

"I'd better get to school," he told Professor Gertie with a sigh. "I've got a *lot* of work to do."

Chapter 4

Harvey spent all Wednesday morning trying to read a history book, while Mr Spottiwoode droned on from the front of the classroom, and Darren talked furiously in his ear.

"Why is he called 'Fly' anyway?" Darren was saying. "He hasn't got six legs, or wings, and he doesn't buzz except when he's blowing his nose."

Harvey shrugged.

"And what's so special about a fly?" Darren went on. "A fly wouldn't be any good in goal. Its wings would get tangled in the net."

"There must be some reason ..." Harvey said as they watched Mr Spottiwoode move slowly around the room with his hands in his pockets. Harvey couldn't imagine him as a professional goalkeeper.

At lunchtime, Harvey had some bad news for Darren. "I'm staying here," he said, piling all his books onto his desk. "I have to study. I've got to try to learn something."

Darren blinked. "Okay," he said. "Me too."

"You don't have to," said Harvey. "You can play a match outside — you're not banned."

"I need to swot as well," Darren said, though Harvey guessed he only wanted to keep him company.

Harvey bent his head over his book.

"I've just thought of something," said Darren, interrupting him.

Harvey tried to read and listen at the same time.

"I think everyone on The Team should get to keep the Floodlights Cup at their house for one week each," said Darren.

Harvey looked up. "Good idea," he said. "But ..." He didn't know how to say it.

"What's wrong with that?" said Darren.

"Nothing," said Harvey. "It's just — I have to study now. I can't talk."

Darren nodded, and Harvey went back to reading his book.

"Wait a minute!" said Darren, grabbing Harvey's shoulder. "Harvey — what was Mr Spot's team called again?"

"They're Finbar Fly's All Stars," said Harvey irritably, not looking up.

There was a silence beside him. Darren was holding his breath.

"What is it?" said Harvey at last.

"All Stars," squeaked Darren. "What does that mean?"

Harvey hadn't thought about it. "It's just a name," he said.

"Or," said Darren, looking terrified, "if Mr Spot used to be a professional, they could be real soccer stars!"

Harvey was aghast. He hadn't even thought about who would be playing on Mr Spot's team. What if they *were* famous players? It was possible.

"There's no way The Team can win against professionals," said Darren morosely.

Harvey felt a stirring inside him. The Team weren't *that* easy to beat — and they never gave in, not even against sides who were bigger and better than them.

Harvey closed his book as the bell went for the end of lunch. He wasn't thinking about history anymore. He was already imagining The Team facing famous players — and beating them.

"We can win if we're ready," he told Darren that afternoon. Mr Spottiwoode had taken the

class outside again, and was making them catch parachutes he dropped from the roof.

Harvey's mind was humming. If only The Team had an advantage. He looked up at Mr Spottiwoode, and saw him rubbing his back as if he was in pain. Aha! "The All Stars will be old, won't they? They'll be slower than us. We can win if we're sharp, focused and fast."

When the bell rang that afternoon, Harvey shoved his books into his bag and ran home. He studied all evening, and even got up early to study before school the next morning.

"It's going well," he told Darren in class. "I've done History and Geography. I'm doing Maths today, and Science tonight. Here." He handed Darren a note, grinning as Darren read it out loud.

"Midweek Report. You, Darren, are BANNED from talking to Harvey until after the test. Yours sincerely, H. Boots."

Throughout that day, Harvey studied for the test, secretly ignoring Mr Spottiwoode's lessons. He had to join in, though, when everyone left their desks, took off their shoes and dragged them across the floor.

"You've not been missing much," Darren told him. "I don't know why we're doing this. If you ask me, Finbar knows you're going to ace the test, and he's so frightened that he can't teach straight."

During the last lesson of the day, Harvey wrote down everything he'd learned so far — and soon had several pages of facts. He began to feel confident. It didn't matter what size his brain was — if he studied hard, he could learn. All he had left to do was Science, and there was just enough time for it after The Team's training session that evening.

"I've got some great new ideas for The Team, too," he told Darren.

Darren covered Harvey's mouth with his hand. "Sshh!"

Mr Spottiwoode was coming towards them.

"I noticed you working at lunchtime," said Mr Spottiwoode. "You're developing good study behaviour, Harvey."

Harvey met his teacher's gaze. He wasn't scared of Finbar Fly, or his All Stars. He was going to be ready for them.

"He's done History, Geography and Maths already," blurted Darren. "He's going to beat the ban!"

Mr Spottiwoode frowned. "You do know that the test is only on *this week's* topic, I hope?"

Harvey's eyes flicked to the blackboard

behind Mr Spottiwoode's desk, and for the first time all week he read what was written on it. "Forces?" he said.

"Correct!" said Mr Spottiwoode. "And thank goodness for that! For a moment I thought you hadn't been taking any notice of my wonderful lessons!"

Mr Spottiwoode walked away, and Harvey stared after him, numb with shock.

"I thought he said *every* topic," Darren hissed. "I was talking to you about the Floodlights Cup while he was telling the class, and I mustn't have heard properly. Harvey, I'm sorry — I got it all wrong."

Harvey turned to Darren. "What are forces?" he said desperately.

Chapter 5

"I won't be playing," Harvey told The Team that evening as they stood under the brand-new floodlights, which would be turned on for the first time on Saturday night. "I studied all the wrong things and the test is tomorrow, so I'll still be banned. But that doesn't mean The Team can't win," he added.

"Yeah, sure, Harvey," said Matt moodily. "The Team are going to beat a bunch of superstars with our striker sitting on the sidelines. No problem."

Harvey lowered his head. Matt had a point, of course. And not only was Harvey The Team's main goal scorer, without him they'd be a player short.

"What did you forget to study?" said Rita.

"Forces," replied Darren.

"Forces!" snorted Steffi. "They're not so hard. Why don't you just read your notes through a few times? You need to put some effort in and ..."

"I wasn't listening," said Harvey. "I was studying other stuff, so I didn't write anything down."

"Didn't you do any practical experiments?" said Rita helpfully. "Like dropping parachutes, and rubbing your shoes on the ground? Or pulling on a rope?"

"I wasn't watching properly," said Harvey.

"This is the Fly's fault," complained Darren. "It's probably all part of his plan to keep Harvey out of the game. Why didn't he stop us talking?"

Steffi rolled her eyes. "If you're at school, you're supposed to pay attention, not wait for someone to tell you to!"

"Your attitude," said Matt, jabbing a finger at Harvey, "has handed our cup to the All Stars on a plate."

Harvey turned away. Matt and Steffi were right. He should have been listening to Mr Spottiwoode all along. That's what school was for.

"Teacher alert!"

Harvey spun around to see where Matt was pointing.

"It's the Fly!" bellowed Darren. "He's come to spy on us!"

Harvey saw someone sprinting towards them so fast his legs were a blur. All he could make out was a suit and tie — but it wasn't their teacher, not unless his eyes had been replaced with laser lights.

"Better late than never!" called Professor Gertie, hurrying after her robot.

Harvey felt a tingle of excitement run up his back. Professor Gertie had *never* let him down before. She would know exactly what to do.

Mark 1 drew to a standstill in front of Harvey. Behind him, he could hear The Team chuckling. The robot was dressed in a brown corduroy jacket, brown shirt and brown spotted tie. Even his trousers were brown.

But it wasn't only his clothes they were laughing at.

"Why's Mark 1 got a moustache?" said Darren.

Professor Gertie ignored him. "I decided Harvey might need some last-minute help to make sure he gets top marks in his test. So I've invented the ultimate solution to everyone's study worries. Let me present ... Mark 2 — the Teacher Machine!"

"Rrrready to rolllll!" chimed the robot, punching the air with both fists.

The Team fell silent. After a minute Rita said, "It's just Mark 1 with funny clothes, right?"

Professor Gertie pursed her lips. "In a manner of speaking," she admitted, "yes. But he's much improved. I have taught him everything I know."

"Can he teach me about forces?" Harvey said eagerly. "I need to learn them — and fast."

Professor Gertie put her lips to the Listener on the side of Mark 2's head and said loudly, "Harvey Forces Teach Fast!" Then she stood back, grinning. "Just give him a moment to prepare himself. Mark 2's head is no longer a space for fishing line and marbles. It is now bursting with useful new circuits, mega-memory chips, nanobotic doo-dahs, and —"

Without warning, the robot's head fell backwards, and a football popped out.

Professor Gertie — and most of The Team — screamed.

The robot bent down, and Harvey saw inside the rubbish-bin head. It was completely empty — except for the Pea Brain. Then the Football Machine's head flipped back into place with a *click*!

"All my effort wasted!" wailed Professor Gertie. "He's got football on the brain!"

"Hey Mark 1," said Harvey. "You're back."

"Heyyy Harvvv," said Mark 1. He put the ball into Harvey's hand. "Let's playyy!"

Harvey dropped the ball to his feet and kicked it towards Rita. "The Team might as well practise," he said dejectedly. "I'll just watch from the sidelines."

"Okay —" Rita began, but as she stooped to collect the ball, Mark 1 snatched it up. He brought it back to Harvey, and began whining loudly in his ear.

Harvey cringed. Mark 1's voice sounded like a badly tuned radio on full volume. It made his head hurt.

Desperate to get rid of the sound, Harvey threw the ball to Steffi. Immediately, Mark 1 leapt towards her, knocked her out of his way, and grabbed the ball again.

"Hey!" yelled Steffi, rubbing her arm. "Professor! Your robot's lost his marbles!"

"Why's he acting like this?" hollered Harvey as Mark 1 screeched at him.

Professor Gertie hung her head. "I don't know, Harvey," she said miserably. "It looks like the Teacher Machine is a failure, and so am I!" Shaking her head sadly, she walked away.

Harvey saw that Steffi was leaving too.

"What about training?" he called, as he watched The Team drift away. He could hardly hear himself over the sound of Mark 1, who was now whirring like a drill. Harvey's head began to throb.

Suddenly, Rita, who'd been watching Mark 1 curiously, ran over and banged the robot three times on the top of his head. Then she screamed into his Listener, "Harvey Forces Teach SLOW AND QUIET!"

"And sso," said Mark 1 gently, "your kick iss the force thatt makes the ball begin to move. Repeat pleaze."

Harvey gaped.

"You'd better repeat it," said Rita.

"My kick is the force that makes the ball begin to move," said Harvey.

"Quite sso," said Mark 1. "And gravity is the force that pulls it downwards to the ground."

"He's teaching you about forces!" said Rita. "I knew it!"

"And I'm learning!" Harvey replied, beaming with relief.

The next morning, Harvey sat at his desk with the test paper in front of him. His fingers were trembling nervously as they gripped a pencil.

Mark 1 had spent all evening teaching him. He'd followed Harvey home and sat with him through dinner. At bedtime, Mark 1 had left, only to return a short time later dressed in pyjamas and carrying a sleeping bag. He continued to talk into Harvey's ear while they both brushed their teeth, and then crouched by his bed, whispering about forces even as Harvey was falling asleep, exhausted.

When Harvey awoke that morning, he'd discovered the robot lying next to him. Harvey had been using one of his feet as a pillow. The Teacher Machine was still and silent at last, and Harvey supposed he'd already told him everything he knew about forces. But had Harvey really learned it?

"Begin," said Mr Spottiwoode.

Harvey started to read through the questions — and his pencil fell to the floor with a clatter.

He didn't know the answers.

His head felt as empty as Mark 1's.

Chapter 6

Harvey could hear Darren scribbling away next to him.

"If I don't know the answer," Darren had told him before the test started, "I'm going to make something up."

I'd better do the same, thought Harvey as he bent over to pick up his pencil.

Something fell out of his ear. It bounced on the classroom floor and, without thinking, Harvey caught it in his fist. It felt prickly. He opened his hand. It was Mark 1's Pea Brain.

No wonder he hadn't been able to wake the robot up before he came to school — Mark 1 wasn't sleeping at all. He was OFF, because he'd given Harvey his *brain*.

Harvey thought about putting it in his other ear to see if it would work there, but he decided not to. He knew that Mark 1 had meant well, but using an extra brain would be cheating — and that was worse than anything, even failing.

Harvey put the Pea Brain on the desk in front of him. He could still hardly believe that everything Mark 1 knew was contained in such a tiny brain. Apart from knowing about forces — and everything else Professor Gertie had taught him — Mark 1 had taught himself to talk, juggle, and even invent things. And on top of all that, he was a soccer genius.

Harvey thought of the amazing shot Mark 1 had been trying to teach him for ages. He had to kick underneath the ball, to make it spin. That way, the air resistance made it move slowly and ...

Harvey sat up in his seat. Air resistance — that was a force, wasn't it? He found the question at the bottom of the page.

What force slows an object as it moves through the air?

Harvey wrote, "Air resistance."

He read the question above the one he'd just answered.

What force pulls objects to the ground?

Harvey wrote, "Gravity." He felt his heart speed up as he answered one question after another. It was like he was skipping past defenders and heading straight towards goal. He was doing it! Soon there was just one question to go and—

"Time's up!" said Mr Spottiwoode and Harvey looked up. The Fly was standing right next to him, watching him. "Please stop writing," he said. "And well done, class."

Harvey put his pencil down as Mr Spottiwoode picked up first Darren's paper, then his.

Harvey felt light and happy. He was sure he'd done well on the test — and now he'd have the chance to beat the best goalie in town.

Chapter 7

In the last lesson on Friday afternoon, Mr Spottiwoode gave back their corrected test papers. Harvey had passed with his highest-ever mark — nine out of ten — and it felt as good as winning a match. Mr Spottiwoode had written, "Excellent. The ban is lifted. But keep it up — winners work hard."

One–nil to me, Harvey thought.

After school, Harvey returned Mark 1's brain and arranged to meet the robot for a training session the next day.

On Saturday, Harvey got up late and spent the afternoon on the field with Mark 1. He was in top form, and when he scored his tenth goal in a row against the robot, his confidence was fully restored. The Team couldn't lose. The cup was theirs.

"I'm ready," Harvey told himself calmly as he walked towards the field on Saturday night. "Ready for anything."

Turning the corner out of Baker Street, Harvey saw that the floodlights were now glowing white and magical in the night sky. A line of children and their parents were walking towards them. Harvey heard a boy say, "I'm going to see Finbar Fly!" and a girl reply, "So am I!"

When Harvey reached the brightly lit pitch, he guessed there were at least two hundred people already gathered. He saw The Team gaping at the size of the crowd. Steffi looked more furious than he'd ever seen her.

"I can't stand it!" she said. "Everyone seems to know what the Fly is, but they won't tell me. Even my teacher knows!"

"Your *teacher*?" said Harvey.

"There's loads of them here," said Darren suspiciously. "If you ask me, we're being set up."

"What for?" said Harvey.

"Think about it," said Darren. "They've got Finbar Fly here to attract a crowd. He's their hero, and they don't want to see him lose. So who do they choose to play against him?"

"Who?" said Matt, scratching his ear.

"Us!" said Darren. "A bunch of kids! We don't stand a chance," he finished sulkily.

Somebody coughed, and Harvey saw that Mr Spottiwoode, hardly recognisable in a silver goalkeeper's jersey, was standing behind Darren.

Darren spun around and goggled at their teacher's huge gloves, then at his even larger boots. Finbar Fly seemed about ten feet tall. The Team looked terrified.

Harvey spoke up. "We do have a chance," he said quietly. The Team all turned to him. "*If* we work hard," he added.

"And that's why I chose you to play against me," Finbar Fly said to Harvey, his moustache bristling in what Harvey took to be a smile. "I know you can work hard when you want to."

The ref blew his whistle and everyone who wasn't playing left the pitch. Harvey saw Professor Gertie and Mark 1 standing on the sidelines. The professor was looking mournful, and Harvey realised he'd forgotten to tell her how Mark 1 had helped him. She probably still thought her Teacher Machine was a disaster.

Rita grabbed Harvey's arm. "Look what we're up against!" she said fearfully.

"What's wrong?" said Harvey, surveying the All Stars. As he'd hoped, they were all old. "Some of them look like they've never played soccer before!" he said. He could feel his heart beating strongly as he waited for the whistle.

Three All Stars attackers lined up right in front of them, before the ref explained that they weren't allowed inside the centre circle. Harvey chuckled. The All Stars were a joke!

"See the tall one with long hair?" Rita said. "That's my teacher, Miss Kwong. Next to her is

Matt and Steffi's teacher, Mr Slack. And that," she said, pointing to a gigantic figure standing like a rock in the All Stars' defence, "is Mrs Quake, our school headmistress."

Harvey looked hard at Finbar Fly's team, and recognised some more teachers from his own school. Darren was right — they had been set up! But their teachers were about to find out how good The Team could be.

"Let's keep the ball to ourselves!" he called to his team mates. "We'll control the game!"

Harvey kicked off to Rita and, with a bellow, Miss Kwong launched herself at them. Rita sidestepped her and knocked the ball to Matt, who passed to Steffi, who sent it gliding back to Darren in goal.

"Short passes, no risks!" Harvey encouraged his team mates.

It was almost like a practice session, Harvey thought. The teachers were wearing themselves out as they chased after the ball, and The Team were soon relaxed and enjoying themselves.

"This is fun!" said Steffi, slipping the ball between Mr Slack's legs and collecting it herself. "We're in charge for once!"

"Mine's very well behaved for her age," commented Rita, giggling as she left Miss Kwong standing.

"I'm giving *my* teacher a gold star!" said Matt, narrowly avoiding being tackled by Mr Slack before he toe-poked the ball to Harvey.

Harvey made his first run upfield — and was promptly flattened by Mrs Quake.

"Sorry, dear," she apologised. "But there *is* a silver cup at stake, after all, and I'm quite determined to win it!"

The teachers began to use their size advantage, barging The Team about in midfield. Harvey was starting to feel frustrated — The Team hadn't had a shot yet. He saw Finbar Fly yawning as he leaned lazily against his goalpost. Time for a test, Harvey decided.

Rita made a run, drawing the defence with her, before back-heeling the ball to Harvey, who saw that Mrs Quake was out of position. Without a moment's hesitation, he whipped a shot towards goal. Skimming low across the grass, it was as far from Finbar Fly as could be.

The legendary goalie took two steps, then launched himself towards it. There was a loud gasp from everyone — even Harvey. Mr Spottiwoode looked like he was flying!

His hands closed on the ball, he rolled over twice, then stood up gracefully and bowed.

But that was nothing compared to what happened next.

Mr Spottiwoode drew back one of his gigantic feet and booted the ball high over

Harvey's head. Harvey twisted around and saw it shining like a shooting star as it sped across the sky. It was heading straight for The Team's goal.

Darren, who was off his goal line, ran backwards, trying to shield his eyes from the dazzling floodlights. He jumped, flapped at the ball, got his fingers to it, lost it, then crashed to the ground as it bounced into the net.

Harvey watched open-mouthed as Mr Spottiwoode cartwheeled towards the corner flag. The ref blew his whistle like a steam engine and called, "Half-time in the Finbar Fly game! Finbar Fly scores!"

The crowd was chanting. "The Fly! The Fly! The Finbar Fly!"

Harvey felt empty. So *that* was the Fly. It wasn't a save — it was a shot.

Steffi marched over to him, her face livid. "Why didn't you know about the Fly? I suppose you and our butterfingers goalie were too busy messing about in class when he told everyone!"

"Nobody at our school knew," said Harvey defensively. "We can still get back in the game though. We need to work harder and —"

"YOU need to work harder," said Matt, poking Harvey in the chest.

"What's that supposed to mean?" said Darren, coming up to stand shoulder to shoulder with Harvey.

"He's *your* teacher," argued Steffi.

"So *you* have to save his shots, Darren," declared Matt.

"And," Steffi ordered, "YOU have to score, Harvey Boots!"

Chapter 8

"Do you ever get the feeling that everyone is against us?" said Rita as she sat down with Darren and Harvey in the centre of the pitch. "Even my dad's hugging Finbar Fly now, and he should be on my side!"

"I'm really, really sorry for letting in that goal," said Darren, thumping the ground with a gloved hand. "I just wasn't expecting it. Do you think you can score?" he asked Harvey hopefully.

Harvey shrugged. "We've got to keep trying," he said.

"The problem is," said Rita, "if you shoot and miss, your teacher will be able to try another Fly."

"I'm ready for him," Darren said in a determined voice. "He only scored last time because I couldn't see."

Professor Gertie came over, her hands thrust deep into her lab coat pockets. "I wish I could help," she said dismally, "but I didn't dare invent anything else in case I made things worse. I'm a complete failure. It might be safer if I give up inventing altogether and become a teacher instead. Like your Mr Spotty."

But Mr Spottiwoode wasn't a failure, Harvey thought. He was the greatest goalie ever, and he'd chosen to become a teacher instead because he'd really wanted to be one.

Harvey remembered that he had something to tell the professor. "Your Teacher Machine was excell—" he began to say, but Professor Gertie had wandered away as Mark 1 came striding towards them.

"She's avoiding him," Rita said. "Doesn't she realise Mark 1's her greatest success?"

The robot opened his mouth and spat two things onto the grass in front of them.

"He's giving me the creeps," grumbled Darren as Mark 1 skipped away backwards. His mouth was still wide open as he sang loudly, "Happee Birth-dayyy, doo doo!"

"We'd better open our presents," said Rita, unravelling a wrinkly yellow baseball cap. "Look at this!" she exclaimed. "Something to shade your eyes, Darren!"

Darren snatched the cap and put it on, calling gratefully, "Thanks, Mark 1!"

Harvey unfolded the second of Mark 1's gifts. It was a white T-shirt which had words written on it in black crayon.

"It looks like my little brother wrote on it," said Rita. "Or someone else who hasn't been to school yet."

Harvey read aloud, "Farts baa wartyup?"

Darren snorted. "No, it's *Farce* ba warty you."

Rita giggled. "It says, *Force be with you!*"

"Well that solves everything," said Darren sarcastically, flinging the T-shirt into the crowd on the way back to his goal for the second half.

Harvey looked around for the rest of The Team. He didn't have time to work out Mark 1's message — he needed to fire up his team mates, who looked like they'd already lost the match.

"Make sure we keep the ball," he urged them. "But this time, we attack!"

Matt clapped slowly, saying, "Great speech — not!"

But the rest of The Team looked like they were willing to try.

As the All Stars kicked off, Harvey noticed the Floodlights Cup was now displayed on a table by the centre line, glittering like a diamond in the light.

Then he took the ball from Miss Kwong as she thundered past him, and began The Team's assault on Finbar Fly.

Don't shoot, Harvey told himself as he neared the All Stars' penalty area. He could have sent the ball bending around Mrs Quake, who was looming in front of him, but to beat Finbar Fly he'd need to be closer.

Mrs Quake barged into Harvey and the ref gave Harvey a free kick. It was still too far out, so he chipped the ball towards Steffi, who was running in. She headed low and central, but Finbar Fly saved it easily with his feet.

The Team piled on the pressure. Rita's wicked back-heel would have fooled any other keeper, but not the Fly. Even Matt joined in, trying a spectacular diving header. Unfortunately, his head connected with Finbar Fly's stomach instead of the ball, and the ref gave him a yellow card.

"Five minutes to go!" shouted Rita's dad.

"Harvey!" called Rita. "We need to score — and now!"

Harvey screwed up his face, trying to think. Everything he knew from playing the game, and all Mark 1's training, was useless against the Fly. What else could he try?

He saw Mark 1 hopping up and down on the sideline. He was wearing the white T-shirt, and pointing frantically at its message.

Farts baa wartyup, thought Harvey. *Force be with you*. His foot provided the force that made the ball move. If only he could kick with more force, the ball would go faster …

Suddenly Harvey realised that there might be one way to beat Finbar Fly. It was time to try something new.

Rita had a corner.

"To me!" Harvey called urgently, and The Team gathered around him.

Harvey quickly explained his idea.

"This had better work," said Matt as they took their positions in front of the All Stars' goal. "Or you've lost us our cup."

Rita jogged across to take the corner kick. She took a run up, and The Team suddenly darted towards her, calling for the ball. As Harvey had hoped, the All Stars followed The Team, while he sprinted back to the goal area to face Finbar Fly alone.

Rita whipped the ball in hard towards Harvey, who saw Finbar Fly spread himself in the centre of his goal, his eyes wide as if he knew what Harvey was planning. Harvey had to kick the ball before it bounced. If he did, *the full force of Rita's cross would be added to the force of his own shot.* Harvey drew back his foot and—

BANG!

He was knocked backwards as the ball rocketed towards goal. Blinking, he watched Finbar Fly explode towards the top corner, his long fingers stretched — but they weren't long enough.

Hardly daring to believe that he had beaten the Fly, Harvey started to raise his hands. And then—

THWOCK!

The ball slammed against the crossbar, and Harvey stared in horror as it bounced onto the goal line — and straight into the waiting hands of the Fly.

Finbar Fly stood up, and fired.

Harvey closed his eyes. This time he couldn't look. He'd been so close to scoring, and now — thanks to another famous Finbar Fly — the All Stars were going to score again.

The spectators were silent. Darren let out a long roar. "Nooooo!" Then the ref's whistle screamed for the end of the game. The Team had lost. And Harvey Boots had failed again.

Chapter 9

Somebody skidded into Harvey, knocking him flat on to his face. He turned over and saw Darren standing over him. Harvey had no idea why Darren was beaming. "What a game!"

"We lost," Harvey told him simply.

"I know," said Darren, looking regretfully towards the Floodlights Cup. He turned back to Harvey. "Shame about that, isn't it?"

Harvey thought the Fly must have hit Darren on the head. "Why are you smiling, Darren?" he said gently.

"Because I feel happeeee!" squealed Darren. "I know the Fly beat me the first time," he explained. "That felt like getting a double detention. But I learned my lesson, and the second time, I was ready for him." Darren clapped his hands above his head. "SWAT!"

"You mean you saved the Fly?" said Harvey.

Darren shook Harvey violently. "Yes! And he's not a bad shot, is he, our Mr Spot? I'm actually quite proud to have him as a teacher. When you think about it, he does try to make the lessons interesting. From now on, I'm going to listen to him sometimes. I think you should too, Harvey."

As Darren carried on telling him how he was going to concentrate more at school, Harvey looked around. The Team were chatting happily with the All Stars as if they'd won, not lost. Harvey couldn't understand it.

Rita came running over. "Harvey, you were brilliant!" she said, chortling. "Did you see how we tricked them?"

"Great shot, Harvey!" said Steffi, kicking one of Harvey's boots as she and Matt walked past. "We've got no complaints."

"It was unstoppable, mate," said Matt, holding out a hand to help Harvey to his feet.

"Darren, Rita," Harvey pleaded. "You *didn't* win a silver cup. None of us did. The Team *failed.*"

"Yeah," said Rita. "But only just."

"You know what I think?" said Darren, chewing his lip thoughtfully. "I think failing now and then is a good thing."

"How do you work that out?" said Harvey.

"Well," said Darren. "You were failing at school, and it made you work harder. Now you know loads of stuff you didn't know before."

"He's got a point," said Rita. "Losing always makes The Team try harder — and get better."

Professor Gertie marched up, with Mark 1 following close behind. "Super game!" she said. "And you did your best, Harvey, your very best. You know, Rita's right. From now on, I'm going to look at my failures as the stepping stones to my wonderful success!" She linked arms fondly with Mark 1, who tried to wriggle away. "Who cares if my inventions don't always do *exactly* what I want them to? My Marky's perfect, just as he is. I'm so proud of him!" She kissed the robot on the top of his head before he could pull free.

Harvey saw Finbar Fly climb on to the table to show off his trophy.

Mr Spottiwoode had *never* failed, thought Harvey. He'd wanted to be a teacher, and he was a good one, too. He even knew how to stop Harvey from failing — by telling him the truth, and making him work harder.

The crowd gasped as Mr Spottiwoode began wobbling dangerously. Then, with a cry, he toppled, dropping the Floodlights Cup. He dived to retrieve it — but missed. A hand Harvey recognised scooped it up, shoved it inside his shirt, and bounded away.

One person began to clap, then another, until suddenly the whole crowd was applauding.

"That kid dives like an *eagle!*" bellowed Rita's dad.

"He's my boy!" said Professor Gertie adoringly, wiping a tear from her eye.

Harvey flung back his head and whooped triumphantly. "Even the Fly's a failure sometimes — he's not perfect!"

"Too true!" said his teacher, springing to his feet. He looked happier than Harvey had ever seen him. "You very nearly beat me. And Darren is one of the few to save a Fly. Congratulations, both of you!"

Harvey saw that Darren was blushing with pleasure.

"Teacher's pets," commented Steffi good-naturedly.

"How about my All Stars play The Team again next year?" suggested Mr Spottiwoode.

The Team, and their teachers, all cheered.

"More failure!" said Darren, rubbing his hands together gleefully. "I can't wait!"

Harvey shook his head, though. In his mind, he saw his shot again, zooming past the Fly's outstretched fingertips. If he had kicked *under* the ball, the way Mark 1 was teaching him, the air resistance would have helped to drop it under the crossbar, and into the net.

"Losing might be good for us," said Harvey. "But next year — we win!"

Prof
Gertie

Darren

Harvey

Rita

Matt

Steffi

Mark 1